Will You Never Forget Me?

Luca Santos

The only affection of the heart for which there is neither assistance nor desire is true love, which is the only heart disease that should be left to "run on."

FIND THE GREAT PATNER

Individuals you, me, we all are basically friendly creatures. Let potentially run wild, we will generally look for each other's organization — intellectually, genuinely, profoundly. You can place few individuals in an enormous space, and in a brief time frame they will bunch, looking to see, hear and contact each other.

It does not appear that being around other people is sufficient. On the everyday level, we, as people, will generally coordinate off looking for more than to simply "hang out" with arbitrary bipeds. We appear to have to experience passionate feelings for, be infatuated and share love. Since we as a whole appear to sort of need exactly the same things, you would figure bringing together and meet each other's common needs would be somewhat simple. But have you ever noticed that the more intelligent and sophisticated we get, the more difficult it seems to be to do the things in our lives that should be easy? I hear from people all the time that, for some reason, they just can't seem to find another person who is willing to share the words "we" and "us," much less put their boots under their beds and start filing joint tax returns. They let me know that they can't get a date and assuming that they do, it's either with some mouth-breather they genuinely want to believe that they at no point ever find in the future or a respectable person who won't get back to, either in light of the fact that he would rather not or is apprehensive his significant other could figure it out. Subsequently, they simply lounge around watching the window hangings blur.

As a couple of portions from your messages and letters show, the majority of you are keeping a comical inclination:

You may be in a better or worse situation than some of those women, but it's time to change things up and get what you really want. To do that you must figure out how to Adore Shrewd.

We are about to significantly alter that if you are unable to fix the guy you got or find the man you want. Assuming that you're up around evening time asking why everyone around you, with the exception of you, is in extraordinary connections, getting ready for marriage, getting hitched, having children and zooming right along throughout everyday life, then, at that point, you and I are going to change that in a significant manner. In the event that you're not finding that unique individual who can illuminate you from the back to front, you are getting bamboozled, and we're certainly going to fix that. There's something off about something. Something is messed up. What aggravates it is that I accept with extraordinary assurance that this unique somebody exists. He is out there. You might have previously met him. You might even be in a relationship with him but are unable to take it to the next level, or you might be married to him but the spark has begun to fade.

To get the relationship you need, you must take a fair, even ruthless, see what's happening and what's turning out badly. You must be willing to alter your activities.

Simply a note to be certain that I'm extremely clear on a certain something: I'm going to let you in on certain mysteries and methodologies, expecting that you have concluded that you need to track down the ideal person for you. I don't currently accept, nor have I at any point accepted, that any lady must be hitched or have a man in her life to be entire, finished or crucially alive. If you find the right man, having a man in your life can be beneficial. It's beneficial to need and have a sweetheart or spouse (not simultaneously, obviously). However, this is not a requirement for you. Getting hitched isn't something you should do.

In this fast-paced day and age in our highly transient society, with its high divorce rate, the task of creating a strong and rewarding relationship may sound intimidating or even overwhelming, assuming that finding the right man is what you want. Allow me to guarantee you, it doesn't need to be. In point of fact, what we are about to do will be more entertaining than the law should permit. Knowing that every day could be the day you meet the person of your dreams, the person with whom you will spend the rest of your life, is so exciting and fun. No one can say with any certainty assuming the following conference you have, the following client you serve or the following corner you turn will place you before that very individual! Because of this, life is thrilling; It doesn't really matter to me what your identity is! Particularly in the event that out of nowhere you are done staggering along carelessly, yet rather have the right stuff, capacities, plans and techniques to get it going! You are going to become amazing at relating. You are about to attain your "black belt" in the relationship. Then you will glance back at what you used to do and simply shake your head.

Allow me to get us going by letting you know two things that I know for outright, drop-absolutely sure. First: on the off chance that you don't have what you really need in a relationship, then you are correct, something is truly off-base. But the crucial part is as follows: The problem is not you. I rehash, the issue isn't you. You are not a terrible individual. You are not neglecting to get a magnificently compensating relationship since you are not deserving of it. As a matter of fact, I accept, to the outright center of my spirit, that you are going to find a colossal mystery, as a matter of fact, I accept it is the trick of the trade in your life: YOU. This mystery isn't just being stowed away from individuals you see consistently, bond with or fantasy about wedding, it is being kept from you.

The second fact that I am absolutely certain of is that you are not thinking clearly or playing the game effectively; if not you would have what you need. We'll manage that in Section 4, "Single — There Are No Mishaps," since you are a meriting and quality potential relationship accomplice, yet you clearly don't have the foggiest idea how to get in the game or play the game once you do.

It is, indeed, a game. Some way or another or another, individuals have concluded that searching for adoration is some massively serious interaction that should be drawn closer with worship and etiquette. I surmise I ought not be so shocked since reality is normally connected with frantic circumstances and "urgency" is a word I frequently hear from all kinds of people in regards to their affection lives. I concur that choosing a soul mate and going with the choice to walk the passageway is a choice of gravity and merits the greatest possible level of in thought, supplication and thought. But getting there is a game, and if you want to win, you have to play it loosely and have fun. You must play the game without sweat-soaked palms or you won't ever get what you are searching for.

Saying that dating and relating is, to some degree to start with, a game doesn't imply that it is unimportant or pointless. Depend on it; I'm looking at rolling out a significant improvement in your life, explicitly your adoration life. Now is the right time to be a champ. Now is the ideal time to begin being a lady rather than a bridesmaid.

Consider it, the issue must be something other than you. Don't you know ladies who are, as you would see it, not quite as intriguing as you, not generally so savvy as you, not as cherishing and mindful and giving as you, not so charming or alluring as you, however yet they have an incredible relationship accomplice while you sit at home conversing with your houseplants? Why? Perhaps they just got visually impaired fortunate, yet I'm wagering they have what they need and what you wish you had on the grounds that they know how to play the game better compared to you do.

I realize that there are additionally ladies out there that you simply love to detest, in light of the fact that they appear to have everything going on. They're youthful, fit, stick-flimsy, lively and charming. You're thinking, "How would I rival that?" You stand in front of the mirror in your bathroom and say, "Look at my hair! Observe my hips! I have legs like stumps! My eyes are excessively far separated! This is the hereditary treachery that is my heritage! I'm bound to kick the bucket alone!" Indeed, wake up! I can guarantee you that you don't need or should be some glamorous lady model that spends her days on the runway. She might be starving at home or throwing up the dinner she just ate, looking in the mirror, and saying the same or worse things as you do. Also, I can't perceive you the number of men that I've heard check out at those ladies and say "For mercy's sake! I've seen more meat on tusks! She requires additional time at the buffet.

Assuming you're sitting at home hounding on yourself with an unending rundown of self-basic put-downs, then, at that point, I ensure that others, including men, will find it undeniably challenging to see esteem in you since you are concealing it so well. As odd as it may sound, before he ever falls in love with you, you will have to first fall in love with yourself. You will need to know and understand yourself.

This is the way this is all going to begin. To get you where you need to go, we will totally modify the content of your life, and you will be the star. We will recognize, portray and embrace the "Personality of You" in Section 3 — and that character will be the star in your life. Furthermore, it's presently not a one-lady show. We will recognize your driving man in Part 2, "The Personality of Him." We will characterize the two characters regarding character, actual attributes, values, convictions and each and every other significant trademark so you know precisely what your identity and you're searching for. You need to know basically everything there is to know about you from the, you need to perceive what your identity is and you need to focus on a "characterized item" of how you will introduce yourself in the social field. The "characterized item " is the most ideal you that is accessible inside the scope of what your identity is, and that is the pony you will ride as far as possible home — right down the walkway. Not any more attempting to be everything to all individuals. Not any more attempting to think about what some man needs and attempting to transform yourself into it. You will be all that you can be, as opposed to someone else, and I guarantee you that will be all that could possibly be needed to make the affection you need.

You will need to identify the aspects of yourself that a man would want. embrace the parts that you don't yet recognize. It ought to be self-evident assuming that you are disrupting yourself. Now that I live in Hollywood, I meet agents everywhere I go. Everybody is trying to get the word out about their undiscovered "star." Imagine if they tried to accomplish that by repeating the same things to themselves about themselves about their future star? Suppose they moved forward and said, "Hello, I got this old stow away of a lady client that I believe you should meet. She's kind of dull and exhausting, doesn't get out a lot and isn't extremely fascinating, at the same time, I don't have the foggiest idea, perhaps you'll like her. She's positively accessible. She hasn't had a date in so long that her clothes are out of style. When you consider the possibility of someone describing another person in that manner, I'm sure that sounds pretty absurd. Assuming this is the case, for what reason doesn't it sound ludicrous to you when you depict yourself that way?

You won't prevail in the profoundly aggressive dating game except if you are persuaded that you are totally awesome.

When you obtain the abilities and capacities important to play the dating game and play it effectively, results will come.

So I'm letting you know that your concern finding the right person doesn't have anything to do with your own value or worth. It isn't so much as an issue of shallow things like your engaging quality. It is, be that as it may, an issue, established in the thing you are doing and not doing. That presumably seems like the terrible news. However, I believe it is simply additional good news given that you can alter your behavior. We are going to assist you with doing that. We're going to tackle your concern, and it won't include a season pass to the plastic specialist or the psychologist. You can meet that one person who is just right for you. You can start a relationship that will satisfy all of your desires and help you realize your childhood ambitions. I'm absolutely serious. If you agree with the ideas I'm about to lay out, do the things I'm going to tell you to do, and use the methods we'll come up with together: solved the issue! It doesn't matter if you can't get a date or the right date, or if you can't get the man in your life to ask you out, or if the man you married doesn't show his love and respect for you. You and I will change all that — and also, we will have an outright ball making it happen. Now is the right time to get what you need!

I don't believe you should frenzy, and I surely don't maintain that you should feel like you've proactively missed the transport, yet the time has come to quit consuming sunlight and to perceive that this is no dress practice. This is Kickoff. Consider this: You're simply going to carry on with a sum of around 25,000 days and no more. That is only 3,900 weeks! Assuming you're in your thirties, you've just got around 12,000 days — 1,800 weeks — left, or 1,800 ends of the week to go to your feline and say, "We should look at what's on Creature Planet." Did you get that? You can gauge what's left of your life in weeks! Weeks! Truly, life can and will travel every which way in a rush. Now is the ideal time to begin playing the game to dominate, and that implies that you need to plan. I've often said that winners do things that losers don't want to do is what separates winners from losers. Now is the ideal time to carry on like a champ.

Here is a primary concern truth: Dating as far as you might be concerned is basically one of the most wasteful, useless, erratic and a mix of good and bad ways of attempting and accomplish one of the main goals of your whole life. When it's all said and done, offer me a reprieve, how weak is regular date manner of speaking: " So what's your sign? Can you believe how much rain we've had? This week, did you read People magazine? Louise, oh my! Before the appetizers arrived, I would be looking for a rope to hang myself from. It's a marvel we haven't vanished as an animal types, inferable from a closure of reproduction. In the event that you go into the dating field, as a great many people, with no preparation, no understanding, no arrangement and no methodology, you're similar to a rocket without a direction framework. You are comparable to a vehicle without a steering wheel. You're just driving around in the hope that Mr. Right will get on the hood, knock on your windshield, and yell, "Hey, stop! It's me, it's me, you tracked down me!" Based on how you've probably been playing the game thus far, I think you'd just hit the wipers and washers to get rid of him like a bug. It's possible that you've already hit him twice! Assuming that is the situation, hopefully he's not a legal counselor!)

I want us to take action, just like the vulture sitting up on a telephone line and telling the other vulture, "Forget this waiting." I'm going to kill something right now. That is how I want you to be. I need you out there getting things going. That's what to do, you really want to have an unmistakable system and you want to have the right stuff to execute that procedure. From getting seen the entire way to finalizing the negotiation. Section 9, "Infrared Dating," will tell you the best way to get to the point with possible accomplices so you're not staying there arranging Harden 0 confines for quite a long time a relationship that never had a future, never got an opportunity to inhale on its own past a couple of irregular great times. In Chapter 7, "Your Man Plan," I'm going to talk to you about where to go to meet potential partners—at a nightclub, gym, church, or online—to find out who is real and who is a waste of time and how to behave when you get there. We'll talk about online dating in Chapter 8, "Fishing with a Net."

Effective dating, on the other hand, is difficult. I can't help thinking about how people at any point get together regardless, not to mention stay together. There couldn't be two more unique "species" on the substance of the planet. I can recollect that when I was youthful, I thought all felines were young ladies and all canines were young men, and that is the reason they didn't get along. After some time, I was able to get that straightened out, but I have to admit that after all these years have passed, I have come to the conclusion that I might have been much closer to the truth when I was five!

A career psychologist like my father used to say that men didn't know anything about women. The day I wedded Robin, he snickered and said there were twice in any man's life that he will be confounded by ladies: before he gets hitched and after he gets hitched. I got the impression that he had not learned this from a book, but rather from difficult life experiences!

Although men and women may not understand each other as well as we would like, I do understand how men think because I am a man. I mean to be like your "companion at the production line." In Section 6, "Your Person Q," we sort out some way to get men to do what you maintain that they should do and not do what you don't believe they should do. My insight is experiential in that I am a man and it's observational in that I have invested a great deal an energy around a ton of folks, some of them dog canines, some of them not. But you need to know what makes a man tick, why he might be afraid of commitment, what he wants, and what it will take for him to see the value in you. If you want to adopt a new last name or hyphenate one you already have, you will need to understand men.

I will zero in not on recondite contrasts, but rather on the things that truly make a difference to you in your mission to track down a man to impart your life to, for example, how to get men to focus on marriage, how to conquer their obvious apprehension about responsibility and how to best guarantee that they esteem you as a lady and treat you with pride and regard.

This will not be an easy deal because men and women have very different priorities, particularly when it comes to starting a committed relationship and getting married. Consider it. Young ladies grow up playing spruce up and having dream weddings. They grow up planning a wedding, acting it out, and covering their heads with towels to look like veils. What do you think men do? We've all heard of the little girls who marry their brothers' G.I. Joes by marching their Barbies down "the aisle." However, have you ever heard of a young boy who broke into his sister's house and stole her Barbie so that she could marry his lonely G.I. Joe? Have you at any point seen a young man destroy tissue paper and put it on a doll's head, imagining that it is a cloak?

When there is such a disparity in priorities, then, what should you do? The response is that you need to make inspiration in your man; you need to make a feeling of want and direness. Similarly as with a great deal of different things, doing that is simple when you know how and it's like attempting to get water to run uphill when you don't. A ton of men have let me know throughout the long term that with regards to dating or being seeing someone, feel they are being pursued, followed and focused on to become spouses. This is somewhat perturbing. You know how ladies generally say that men are keen on just something single. I can assure you that men have their own version of that tale; men believe that you, too, are only interested in one thing. The objective is to make a need to get moving without the impression of tension. I suppose there is some symmetry there because men and women both believe there is a clear cause-and-effect relationship between what they want! And keeping in mind that marriage may as a matter of fact be your essential goal, you super aren't that a very remarkable danger to a man who thinks he esteems his "opportunity" — in light of the fact that, to be perfectly honest, I think most ladies just aren't truly adept at finalizing the negotiation. Face the facts: It is time to rectify the situation if you lack technique. I will show you how in Part 10, "Pack them, Tag them, Bring them back Home." On the off chance that you will make a genuine association with a man, trap him, yet catch his heart, brain and soul AND make him like requiring some serious expertise — you're going.

Desperation without pressure is the objective. Explicitly you really want to know how to track down the perfect man, draw in him, persuade him and wed him. That is gruff, however if that is the thing you need to realize that is the thing we will do and live it up while we're making it happen.

In the event that you're as of now hitched to a man, and you simply need to re-get those fires going and keep them consuming, you also will require the serious expertise from Part 11, "The Province of Your Association."

This book isn't tied in with tracking down Mr. Perfect At this point; it is tied in with tracking down Mr. Perfect. I say that since a tremendous contrast between is having the option to get a man to say "I do" at a given second in time and having the option to get him (or you) to say, "I'm joyfully hitched as long as possible." On the off chance that you want to get to "I do," you have an alternate arrangement of guidelines from what you have on the off chance that your objective is "I'm." To get to "I do" you simply let a man know anything he desires to hear just to inspire him to say those words and stroll down the path. You can then zero in on the significant issues of contending with your mother about food providers and photographic artists. Yet, you won't be cheerfully hitched. Indeed, you'll get your fantasy day, however you will miss the mark concerning a fantasy life. On the off chance that you're searching for over an extended period of wedding arranging, an extravagant dress and a major party; on the off chance that what you need is a strong relationship in view of a groundwork of adoration and mindful; If what you want is more than just an "I do," but rather a sincere and resolute "I am happily married," then closing the deal is not about finding any man but rather about developing a relationship with the right man that will benefit you both. Presently how about we get everything rolling.

CHARACTER ASSESMENT

The signs are everywhere: Your natural clock is ticking boisterously to the point that your neighbors can hear it; your stomach presumably turns at the possibility of going to another noisy, smoke-filled bar just so a lot of folks can stare at you like a twenty-ounce porterhouse (with a heated potato as an afterthought); also, you're believing, "In the event that I need to continue even another date with another hair-gelled, shades around evening time wearing nice guy who spends more on garments than I do, I will hurl in my mouth." Assuming that is you and you need off the dating circuit, it is the ideal opportunity for you to quit behaving like a position novice, only looking and hanging tight for an irregular person to pick you. In the event that you will adore shrewd, you must date savvy. You've that is old news — it's the ideal opportunity for the following period of your life to start.

Then again, you might be the sort who never goes on dates or to clubs. You're an untouchable who couldn't actually sort out some way to get into the game to the point of being tired of it, significantly less the way in which you'll at any point find the person you need. You've watched Sex and the City and believed it's a fantasy — "No chance are there ladies out there who are dating as much as these four," not when your last date was the point at which the macarena beat out all competitors! I'm with you there. Like such a large amount what you see on TV or on the big screen, that show and others as it mirror no world I've known about. To that end such countless individuals watch them, wishing life truly could be like that. Perhaps you're like that. Perhaps you've lived vicariously through each celebrity and lighthearted film you can imagine and you've had it up to your ragged looking eyeballs with watching the world go by.

Whether you're a "no need to relive that" lady or an "I don't actually have the foggiest idea how to arrive" lady doesn't exactly make any difference much. The two sorts of ladies are in almost the same situation. Whichever you will be, you haven't had the option to get a traction on a quality relationship with a quality person. Furthermore, that isn't on the grounds that you're a failure, but since you haven't exactly gone at this like a victor — with the arrangement and range of abilities important to boost your possibilities.

Men ought to be like Kleenex — delicate, solid and expendable.

Therefore, here we are. We should get down to what's really going on with this part — composing a person profile of "him." Who precisely, definitively, explicitly do you view as a quality person? Sorting this out now doesn't imply that you ought not be liquid and open to change, yet it serves to essentially begin considering some goal. I won't attempt to transform you into some high-upkeep, hyperpicky downer. I simply need to assist you with halting kissing frogs and begin tracking down your man. Here is where we set a few norms and begin figuring out how to dismiss those folks who fall such a long ways underneath the bar that they do right by prisoners. This is tied in with starting in view of the end (as Dr. Stephen Flock would agree) and not messing with a dog canine when what you truly need is somebody with a family — or in any event, somebody who's housebroken and will not chew on the furnishings!

Furthermore, kid, are there a great deal of dog canines out there. A lady was letting me know as of late about this person who was coming on major areas of strength for super attempting to deeply inspire her at a retreat in Aspen, Colorado. James Bond, in comparison, was modest when he heard her tell his story. She said in the event that he'd been any more brimming with himself, she would have needed to get a table for three rather than two just so his self image wouldn't need to stand.

It appeared that he was regaling her with tales of all the status symbols that he cherished as his own: his Porsche stopped out front; his new Reach Wanderer, which was being hand-waxed back at his carport; his gold Rolex, which he kept on flashing in case she missed it. He talked about his Prada shoes and his craft assortment. No disgrace — his tall structure apartment suite, his boat in the marina, he forgot about nothing. The person had no disgrace — like a server glad for himself for having impeccably discussed the specials he wrapped it up with a priggish look that appeared to say, "So what is your take?" She looked at him dead without flinching and expressed, "Need to understand my thought process? I think you have a great deal of bills, Smooth. You either possess more cash than brainpower or you are in hawk up to your eyeballs." Absolutely unmoved, she had been staying there the entire time pondering, "What's going on with young men and their toys! I would never, ever spend money on that junk! Jeez, what might be said about a school reserve for my kids, a retirement record, investment funds and a spouse who spends more on his family than his golf clubs? That is my wish!"

See, I comprehend the allure of the dog canine. I've already heard that old boys' song and dance numerous times. You must comprehend: It's not always the characteristics of a man that make him a good long-term partner that initially draw you to him. Assuming you are really hoping to settle down you actually don't comprehend that the person pursuing you may not be the individual you need bringing up your kids or being there for you through various challenges, then it's time we get you an arrangement, a profound compass, and begin changing your choice measures right away.

Is there anything wrong with someone who is attractive, supercool, good at dancing, and fun on dates? Definitely not. In point of fact, you might think that those conditions are necessary, and they might be, but that doesn't mean that those characteristics are enough to support what you want.

I don't mean for this to sound like a boring job because, as I mentioned in Chapter 1, this should be an exciting process. But we might as well make sure you're having a good time with guys who have a chance of being "the one" at least. As a result, you should stop spending time with people you absolutely, positively, and positively know will not lead you anywhere. You shouldn't go barhopping because you're afraid of being alone.

In the event that you need what you need when you need it and what you need is a genuine, no doubt about it, quality accomplice and when you need it is presently (or yesterday before early afternoon) rather than a long time from now or never, then you would rather not befuddle capricious social movement with social efficiency.

Here is a demeanor change for you: Conclude right now that you would prefer to be content alone than hopeless with another person. Conclude that you won't pick some person out of dread that you may not get a superior decision later. For instance, unless you're writing a country song, you won't benefit from a guy you know who drinks excessively, has a difficult personality, and despises children. He might be a good time for the evening, yet there's no possibility for a future since he has bargain breaking qualities or values. Even if it means going home alone, you need to pay attention to those and knock on the door.

I know Debbie, a 34-year-old woman who was dating a guy she was insanely attracted to. We're talking catnip. That is to say, she could and did effectively go through hours simply gazing at his image and staring off into space about how provocative he was. However, regardless of all that mooning, she kept a piece of herself down and never let herself get excessively connected. She kept her equilibrium by seeing others since she had been scorched by enchanting "nice guys" previously and realize that once the physical allure settled down, she would be left with an attractive and beguiling person who was likewise incredibly youthful, controlling, reserved and untrustworthy. Sat around! He was only an interruption, taking important time that might have been gainfully enjoyed with genuine conceivable outcomes. She left him a long ways behind.

On the off chance that you haven't halted to give your necessities and needs some serious idea, you presumably wouldn't know Mr. Perfect on the off chance that he approached you wearing an ID. You don't fit with everyone, and not every person fits with you. There are individuals out there who will make you insane as well as the other way around. I need to ensure that you have a reasonable vision of what you need and what you don't need — what you totally can't live with versus "Indeed, this is the establishment on which I can fabricate a future."

A hint for you: What you need isn't be guaranteed to Brad Pitt, George Clooney, Gandhi and Bill Doors generally moved into one. All things considered, as he progresses in years, he's probably going to have Bill Doors' looks and Gandhi's cash. You're not going for some fantasy fellow here, in light of the fact that going for a fantasy fellow is an effective method for pardoning yourself from the game — just set the bar so high that no one estimates up, then, at that point, shrug your shoulders and say, "That is the reason I'm distant from everyone else." No, we are going to enter the room and be realistic in order to locate someone who might be the right kind of guy. Then we'll make the right sort of involvement.

101 Deal Breakers: When describing his character, it's just as important to say what you don't want as what you do want. Thus, first we should make a fast rundown of what you don't need and totally won't endure. These are what I call issues. They are the attributes, characteristics and qualities that conflict

with your basic beliefs: that arrangement of standards and convictions — like genuineness, equity and fortitude — which you use to pass judgment on character and moral fiber and which effectively keep up with your honesty. In the event that somebody has qualities that obviously opposed this basic belief framework, it doesn't a lot matter how charming you think he is or how decent a vehicle he drives. Assuming there is something about him that you realize will drive you out of your consistently cherishing mind quickly by any means, then you really want to resolve that issue on the spot.

Trust me, assuming that you're managing a person who is broken in some significant manner, advise him to find support, provide him with the name of a decent guide however don't take that on when you actually have a choice to shrewdly pick. Although it may sound harsh, you are seeking a partner who is healthy, functional, and uniquely compatible with you. You are not a shelter, you're not Ms. Fix-It and, in any case, he as of now has a mother! Assuming you are hitched or profoundly infatuated or both and your accomplice has created serious defects and issues, that is something else. You are at an alternate stage. You've promised to show up for him, to help and guide him, to calmly assist him with recuperating what troubles him, however not with the eventual result of being pointless.

Taking on large issues, be that as it may, is simply stupid. Don't think that being a rescuer and earning your place will help you succeed. Consolidating two lives without problems like that is sufficiently intense. You genuinely deserve a completely working, solid, quality mate. You must beginning settling on various decisions, and that implies at this moment: Unless you're starting a rock band, no wounded, crazy, or broken-winged men, alcoholics, or drug addicts are required to apply. No harmful, impolite jerks who are decent one moment and mean the following, and afterward come slithering back in a winding of culpability. These folks are not prone to improve, and on the off chance that they do, it should accompany proficient assistance and not on your life.

The good news is that you don't have to take the guy who violates your core values because there are enough people out there—enough fish in the sea—who don't. It's the clearest rule on the planet: Try not to pick the person who is broken. It resembles purchasing a vehicle. On the off chance that two vehicles are staying there, and one has been destroyed while the other doesn't have a scratch on it, hell, even Lassie knows to pick the one that isn't harmed.

So close to the undeniable issues that we recently talked about, what are your own issues? Assuming you are truly strict and wedding somebody outside your religion is something you can't manage, simply don't go down that walkway. In the event that really focusing on your family and investing energy with them is a major piece of your life, however he likes to invest time alone with you, that is a family fight holding back to detonate. This kind of relationship usually ends in heartbreak. In the event that you are searching for significant eye to eye connection, however he'd prefer gaze at his appearance in the mirror looming over your head, then you might have an egotist on your hands. On the off chance that you distinguish even a smidgen of instability, give careful consideration. Do bar brawls will quite often chase after him? Does he struggle with remaining calm? I've frequently said the best indicator of future way of behaving is significant past way of behaving. So check the person's set of experiences out.

Try not to feel that you are such a powerful female power that you are the person who can tame the monster. In the event that he has been hitched three or multiple times, has had four illicit relationships (that you know about), can't hold a task and is monetarily flippant, then he really wants a sedative firearm, not a sweetheart. He might be adorable and enchanting, yet on the off chance that he beverages, battles and bets, continue to walk. I know that sounds so clear I ought not be throwing away life on it, however we both know individuals, perhaps you, who simply don't appear to be ready to stay away. You can't pick a person whose core values, traits, or characteristics compromise you because there are too many fish in the sea. Once a suitable fish is placed in your boat by us, you are free to gut, clean, and fry it however you please. Obviously, this is a joke, but you will have options!

Presently I've gone through and provided you with a short rundown of issues worth considering, and you might have others. When those are found, they turn into stop signs. Put them on your "launch" list and simply don't go there.

The Experience of You

I believe you should expect briefly that
you have found someone who rings your
ringer, gets your fire going and gets your
engine running — all simultaneously. We
should simply expect you've found him
and he is absolutely a willing soul. Let me
know how you feel, realizing that this
individual is blindly enamored with you?

Is it safe to say that you are feeling a
feeling of having a place? A feeling of
acknowledgment? Is it true that you are
feeling fortunate, honored and pleased
with yourself and of your accomplice? Do
you feel harmony, bliss, security? Do you
believe you have at last found your place
in this world through this individual with
whom you will share you life?

That is the very thing that you truly need
— those sentiments and not the
personality of him are your genuine
objective. So for what reason would we

say we are going to go through the most common way of fostering the Personality of Him? Since those are the attributes and characteristics prone to make this feeling we have quite recently depicted. So while you really must have a list of things to get, it's similarly critical to recollect that you're truly searching for the person that will give you the inclination. Also, brace yourself for what I'm about to tell you, when you discover that inclination, you won't really mind what covering it comes in.

For example — and I can express this with very nearly 100% sureness — scarcely any tall ladies grow up longing for wedding a person who's scarcely sufficiently tall to continue every one of the rides at a carnival or requirements a stepladder to change a light on a work area light. Truth be told, the main thing that the greater part of the single tall ladies I know ask while considering a prearranged meeting is, "How tall would he say he is?" In any case, to the extent that tall wedded ladies go, their spouses arrive in various sizes. Also, accept me, the tall young ladies who wedded short folks aren't lounging around reviling their destiny. A long way from it.

Finding genuine affection is as much about you as your accomplice. Ask yourself: What do you desire? A dearest companion who fulfills you," "Somebody you can't survive without," "An individual with whom you need to share" . . . Notice that there's a great deal of "you" in there since genuine romance, regardless of whether you feel it, depends on you. It truly is a decision.

What's more, I would rather not make this excessively clinical, in light of the fact that I realize there is some science included and lightning strikes what not. I see that. I truly do. However, on the other hand, a lot of it comes from thinking, "You know what? I will sprout where I'm planted. This is where I am, so I will focus on this and I will make it happen."

Furthermore, don't allow yourself to be allured by his attractive features; he needs to cause you to feel the manner in which you need to feel. Actual traits that appear to be so significant at the outset become shallow. Level, weight, hair tone, work and that large number of kinds of things that might have drawn in you to him at first and made your chest expand proudly when you stroll into a party together will be at the lower part of the rundown depicting the Personality of Him. That is on the grounds that what you are searching for is the experience of you and not the Personality of Him. What's more, the things that will make this for you will be his qualities, character style and connection style, and the manner in which he assists you with feeling.

We will distinguish the Personality of Him to give you a few rules. However, whether he's short, tall, calm, unconstrained or easygoing, the main thing is what you feel when you are around him. Is your inclination going to be sufficient? " You respond, "Well, geez, I feel that way with this alcoholic here." You might feel as such now, it might ring your chime today, yet it won't in the long haul, and for that reason you will require the rules we recognize in this section.

The 80% Arrangement

Allow me to provide you with a fair warning: On the off chance that you assume you have met Mr. Great, you really want to insult yourself or scrub down, since you are entranced. The 100% up-and-comer doesn't exist. Truth be told; the ideal fit is a fantasy straight up there with effortless dentistry and easy waxing. In the event that you truly accept there's an ideal fit, you're presumably as yet checking your directives for that person you met at a club last year who guaranteed he'd call. Assuming you think you've tracked down the ideal man, don't yell it from the housetops. Return home, settle down and accept it as a sign that people in love don't care about the details and you are messing with yourself.

Everything I'm saying to you is that as opposed to with nothing to do looking for a careful match, search for the person who is liberated from the issues and has 80% of what you truly do need in an accomplice. The other 20% you can develop. Assuming the person has 80% of what you need and potential to develop the additional 20%, you really want to pack that kid up on the grounds that he is all set. Try not to stroll past him while you're searching for Mr. 100%, in light of the fact that another person will wed Mr. 80% and you will be remaining there 60% miserable and 40 percent baffled.

I've guided many couples and I've been companions with many couples and I will let you know that in the entirety of my years as a companion, specialist and person cooperating on the planet, I still can't seem to stumble into the "ideal couple." That ideal couple is a fantasy, so don't burn through your time attempting to turn into the first. Am I advising you to think twice about? Indeed, obviously I'm. Life is a split the difference. Connections are a split the difference. Does that mean you ought to abandon the 20% you could do without? No way. You work on it. What's more, assuming all you at any point get is 80% of that missing 20%, take my statement, you will be hitched and glad for quite a while.

At last it boils down to the contrast between individuals who don't joke around about responsibility and individuals who are out pursuing a dream — the previous will happily neglect the blemishes of a 80 percent accomplice for the present, though the last option will continue to look until they sort out that a 100% match is probably essentially as genuine as 100 dollar Rolex.

Spouses Limitless

Since you're two sections into this book, I figure that you fully intend to take care of business and I need to give you the devices you want to assist you with tracking down your join forces with least experimentation. Champions have a method called perception, by which they really see and feel what it resembles to win before they've even begun the game. You've proactively portrayed what it might feel want to have what you need in the segment of this part headed "The Experience of You." Presently, we will imagine the individual who will cause you to feel that multitude of magnificent, blissful feelings that will accompany being important for a couple.

Envision that we are making a film of your life. Your responsibility is to compose a magnificent content about how you believe your story should unfurl, especially your heartfelt story line. The main thing you'll need to do is depict your driving man, a.k.a. your future spouse. I maintain that you should be very unambiguous while imagining this man. That's what to do, you might have to ponder the sorts of male characters you've found in your life. How about we play some original film jobs similarly as specific illustrations (these are neither genuine individuals nor great "measuring sticks," yet I use them as models since we both know them): Tom Hanks is your delicate dream fellow in Restless in Seattle. He is a closest companion, a dad, a nurturer. He's entertaining and dry — the sort of fellow who can find a place with any gathering. On the opposite finish of the range is Richard Gere in Lovely Lady. He plays serious areas of strength for a magnate — rich, strong and ordering. He is liberal and steady, refined and modern — a man who accompanies a way of life. Then, at that point, you have your enthusiastic and sincerely expressive sort in Screwy: Nicholas Enclosure. This person is the pith of intensity and science. At the point when he needs you, you know it, and neither downpour, nor snow, nor hail nor slush will prevent him from pursuing you. The rundown goes on, yet the characters are totally obvious, and assuming you remember them you realize they had explicit attributes that went a long ways past the short portrayal above.

That is the manner by which exact I maintain that you should be while envisioning your future spouse. You must ponder what you need intellectually, genuinely, inwardly, occupationally, socially, mentally — everything that make you say, "Gee, presently there's a person I wouldn't see any problems with going through my time on earth with." Assuming that you're circumventing saying, "I'll know it when I see it," I have news for you: The main thing you will see is every other person meeting the right person. So we should not squander one more moment. Let's determine the kind of man you want right now.

Go through the accompanying five records and circle all that you can envision as a beneficial quality in your extraordinary somebody. Relax assuming your list of things to get appears to be excessively lengthy. Circle however many things in every class as you want. Ponder you, your life and your likely focuses as you go. Which characteristics could get you all worked up? Which ones will make your life simpler? Furthermore, which ones have you been searching for from the start?

Social style: This is about how you need your fantasy fellow to connect with you. Could it be said that you are keen on someone who believes you should be his beginning and end and remembers you for every one of the plans he makes? Or on the other hand could you lean toward a different and confidential life and wouldn't fret a different get-away every so often? Do you need a heartfelt who says and does characteristically heartfelt things? Let me tell you, if you marry a man who doesn't have it in him and needs a love letter every week, you could be disappointed for years. The equivalent goes for nurturing styles. Do you prefer a man who will take responsibility for that, or one who will delegate child rearing to you?

What about the topic of money, too? What is Mr. Wonderful's position regarding the significance of finances in a relationship?

Does he trust that it's a monetary association, meaning it's "our" cash and we will present on all choices, or does he like to assume the weight of liability regarding the monetary preparation? Do you need a person who needs a pleasant house, a three-vehicle carport, a beefed up sound system, the most recent television, refreshed kitchen machines, the works, or somebody who doesn't take an excess of confidence in material features?

Then, at that point, you have your sexual issues. Do you need somebody who is profoundly charged, or is once a month fine and dandy by you? Are you a traditional or sexual vixen? In this regard, you must know what you want. If you and your partner are sexually compatible, your relationship will have more chemistry, heat, and intensity.

Think about how your ideal man would treat you in a relationship, and then write down the descriptions that come to mind.

graph Sincerely expressive. Expresses his sentiments.

outline Tender. Shows feeling through much love.

chart Heartfelt in every one of the ways Trademark would anticipate.

diagram Model of active involvement in parenting.

outline In charge of funds.

diagram Willing to share financial responsibility.

diagram Extremely sensual

diagram Not sexual at all.

outline Reserved and doesn't need or offer a lot of consideration.

diagram Compassionate while remaining objective.

chart Cash propelled and a hard worker who should have all the common luxuries.

diagram A solitary bohemian who does not require many creature comforts.

outline Somebody who adamantly requests to get everything he could possibly want.

outline Open to think twice about.

chart Indivisible from you.

outline Needing a great deal of individual space.

outline Profound similarity: Regardless of whether you are strict, the truth of the matter is that ideally you would presumably like your accomplice to concur with your view on this. Or not. Perhaps you'd prefer have a home with different viewpoints. Whatever your situation, once more, it's ideal to understand what you need going in. Profound convictions are profoundly imbued during our childhood, and the opportunity that somebody will go from a prized conviction framework isn't perfect. Positively, individuals are much of the time brought back to life, however in the event that you're a reliable Christian, perhaps you shouldn't wed a skeptic and petition God for a supernatural occurrence until the end of your life. That is the meaning of disappointment.

Investigate the accompanying rundown and verify whichever way to deal with otherworldliness works for you.

chart He is exceptionally perceptive of a similar religion as you.

chart He is to some degree perceptive of a similar religion as you.

outline He isn't the slightest bit perceptive, yet comes from a similar strict foundation as you.

graph He isn't in any way shape or form strict yet has confidence in a higher power.

diagram He has no faith whatsoever in a higher power.

outline It doesn't make any difference what he accepts for however long he is liberal and aware of your convictions.

chart Actual attributes: Presently we should conclude what you'd like Mr. Astonishing to seem to be. Is he required to be a large man? Or on the other hand perhaps you're modest and you need a more modest person? Is it true or not that he is athletic? Does he have to have hair? (Heads up!) Provided that this is true, do you like brown, fair or red hair? Certainly, this might appear to be shallow; also, no doubt, you likely could think, "What difference does it make? so long as he has everything else I want?" It all makes sense to me, yet humor me. It's most certainly not by any means the only thing — it's not so much as something critical — yet it's essential for the equation you get. So go on, fill in or circle what you'd need assuming that you had your druthers.

graph Hair tone, hairdo.

depiction of eye color

depict Age

depict Height

chart Body type: athletic, thin, strong, normal size.

chart Pleasant voice.

That was the tomfoolery part. At least on paper, you now have your 80 percent guy. Presently comes the crucial step. Whenever you blend two lives, there is continuously going to be some agony of change. You must forfeit a portion of your time, space, cash, exertion and opportunity — and you surely must think twice about some of what you need.

Now that you're through orbiting your needs, revisit your decisions and cross off all the extravagance things you can manage without. What's more, I amount to something that can fall into the 20% of the 80-20 equation. What remains is your norm. Even if the guy who fits this description doesn't immediately pique your interest, if you let him get you away from your TiVo, you might just end up having a great time.

Get Serious Now, go over your needs list once more. Is it still excessive? Is everything an unquestionable requirement? Have you ruled out split the difference? Is it safe to say that you are restricting yourself with your elevated expectations? Find opportunity to think about your decisions previously. Or, if you absolutely have to, think about the cell phone that is no longer ringing. What are the issues? On the off chance that your rundown is as long as my arm, I know why no men are calling — you're more elite than the celebrity room at the Vanity Fair Oscar party!

This is an ideal opportunity to put on a few optics and look somewhat more profound into the field of competitors. Let's assume you want a vehicle. You need power situates however you must have cooling. Now, let's say you can't afford either. Is it safe to say that you will use whatever might remain of your days strolling to work or would you say you will manage your rundown? So suppose you meet a person who has the genuineness and the desire. Perhaps you can figure out how to live without the funny bone.

You have the opposite issue if all the wrong men are calling you. You are not being sufficiently selective. Mass promoting can be exceptionally rewarding — in the event that you've thought of an extraordinary new item for putting away extras. However, if you promote your highly sought-after companionship, you might be underselling yourself. You will be overwhelmed with demands and have no savvy method for picking and pick. One young woman I know stays at home about twice a month. I'm not joking with you. She is out constantly, either with her companions or with some person. In any case, one of the makers I work with invests energy with her, and the manner in which she tells it, it's a quite sorry sight. When asked, the girl will go out with anyone. Hell, even drive-through joints don't give everybody access. These two ladies have raised a ruckus around town together, and the maker tells me, "You might have a hard time believing the failure that was hitting on Marisol the previous evening. Be that as it may, get this — she really gave him her number. Her genuine number." The young lady has no channel. Anyone who asks her will go out with her. She's very nearly thirty years of age, however she's still as frantic for consideration as a five-year-old.

So check your rundown out. Is it, truth be told, excessively short? You might have been a bad equal-opportunity dater. Also, perhaps at this point, you're beginning to accept that all men are washouts since you meet such countless unseemly ones. Lady, you need to put some barriers around yourself if you selected less than five characteristics from that wish list. Compared to community colleges, you might be easier to get into. Have a few limits. Learn about your true preferences. And don't just listen to the part of you that can't stand being on your own. Try not to be the young lady who would prefer to have a date, any date, than go through a night with a hot shower and a decent book. When you do that, you accidentally make yourself alone, or at least in company with the wrong people, which can be very lonely.

Moving on Now that we've talked about what you want in a man and what you know you won't stand, you know who you want. More significant, notwithstanding, you've understood that you can't become amped up for a list of references or a worked out rundown of characteristics. What gets you moving is the possibility of an organization with somebody you regard and need to invest energy with, and the feeling of having a place and satisfaction that this person gives.

Your goal is to have that warm, fuzzy feeling of being a part of a couple. Not a guy who meets all of your requirements and wears the suit. There are a lot of guys who fit the bill, but it takes time to find the guys who help you feel and give you the experience you want. But the search will be much simpler for you now that you know what you want.

SOCIAL LIFE

On the off chance that you're similar to the a large number of ladies I've conversed with, you're likely reasoning there are a great many hot, youthful, single young ladies and every one of the heroes are taken or gay — or perhaps both. You're giving it your best shot to keep up. Cost-effective haircuts? Check. trips to all of the right places to vacation? Twofold check. A gym subscription? Hanging out at the objective rich conditions also called "in vogue dance club" or "new eatery bars"? Check, check, check. Nevertheless, you feel like you're wearing yourself out, running on a treadmill and wasting time quick and perspiring simultaneously. You're lounging around scratching your head and pondering, "What's going on with me? Why her and not me? Is this a type of dog biscuit? For what reason might I at any point appear to get a person to save my life while that young lady who is unkempt, messy, smokes and has five piercings in her lip is strolling connected at the hip with what resembles Jude Regulation's more youthful sibling! or a guy who doesn't look very good but looks pretty cool.

I don't have any idea how to address that particular inquiry, since I don't have any acquaintance with you. It's possible that people see something wrong. Perhaps they think you look, act or smell entertaining, I don't have the foggiest idea, however I'm wagering it's none of those three things. I won't mess with you: It's a cruel dating world out there, and if you have any desire to win and have your desired relationship you must raise your game. Yes, it is, in my opinion, "a game," at least at this level and stage. I know, I know, I can hear some of you with all the progress of Auntie Honey bee saying, "Indeed, Andy, I don't think finding a soul mate to go into the holiness of marriage is any sort of a game. So there." All I can perceive you is that you're not strolling down the passageway right now, so ease up around 1,000 percent and have a great time!

Men and women have been "playing the game" and "doing the dance" for centuries in the highly competitive social market. It doesn't debase the interaction in the event that you play with trustworthiness and are what your identity is. You must first understand who you are and then commit to being that person.

So how are you going to go from remaining uninvolved and watching others score to taking the ball to the circle yourself? How are you going to get off the never-ending dating merry-go-round, where one cool jerk after another can't even commit to a hairstyle, let alone a relationship with you? Truly, what are you going to do — shy of moving to Gold country, joining a brotherhood or finding a new line of work on the floor of the stock trade where the chances are ten to one in support of yourself?

First of all, I'm going to let you know that you probably have it right: It's possible that Carole in accounting isn't any funnier, prettier, or cooler than you. The explanation you've spent the last four Friday evenings staring at the television with your feline while her end of the week evenings are reserved a long time ahead of time is that she is better — better at the game. I've said it multiple times, "It is possible that you get it or you don't." What you really want to get is what's genuinely going on with this section — how to recognize the best-quality Person of You. That implies being straightforward with yourself about your assets and shortcomings, which isn't simple all the time. It very well may be difficult to concede that you may some of the time be timid or controlling, or anything your shortcomings might be, however knowing and tolerating them gives you a certainty that can't be faked. This awareness also enables you to comprehend how those characteristics may, in the short or long term, turn people off and how you can control them to prevent them from interfering with your relationships.

Whenever you've distinguished and embraced all aspects of the Personality of You, you can put whichever qualities you wish out into the world as a characterized item. Take me, for instance. You are aware of what you are getting when you watch the Dr. Phil show, purchase a Dr. Phil book, or attend a Dr. Phil speech because it is a clearly defined product. Being a direct, straightforward, in front of you portrayal of reality is going. That is the characterized item that is Dr. Phil. In any case, that is definitely not a full portrayal of my Personality of You. There is so much more, like my husbandism, fatherhood, and involvement in my church community; what I for one accept and esteem; You don't get to see everything in my life story every time. Yet, anything specific setting you experience me in, what you really do get to see is a genuine subset of my Personality of You. It's real, it's me, and it's true, but what I choose to say is appropriate for that circumstance.

The Personality of You is the wide and comprehensive meaning of who you are from the back to front, while the characterized item is anything side you decide to show in a given social circumstance. Presently beyond a shadow of a doubt: After you've concluded that this is the pony you will ride through the race called life, your whole involvement with the social, dating and making a-relationship field will change for eternity.

In the event that You Couldn't Date You, Who Might?

I'll say it again because it's important to say: The principal individual you need to offer yourself to is you. That is the significant initial step to distinguishing the Personality of You. I call it characterizing your own reality — it's what you tell yourself when no other person is looking. Assuming you're let everybody know that you're the best thing since the iPod, however where it counts inside you accept you are an eight-track player or the "rotund young lady" who couldn't get a man with a net and a pack of hunting canines, then you're setting out toward additional evenings alone than a sheltered religious recluse. You will produce the outcomes that compare to your own reality.

I mean that. I don't care how well-crafted your argument or presentation are; in the event that you have a messy individual truth, you can seem to be Miss Universe as far as I might be concerned. If deep down, you accept you're carrying on with a major untruth since you're simply a loathsome outcast who is bound to meander the planet alone, individuals will detect it instantly and run the alternate way. They will figure, "Hello, she understands herself better than any other person, and in the event that she believes she's useless, why should I contend? See ya!" Or on the other hand perhaps you'll discover some failure who doesn't mind who he's with or what your identity is, just inasmuch as he has someone — anyone. That is not the very thing you need by the same token. You merit better. Trust me when I say that being with someone is very different from being with just one person. You are destined to end up with the leftovers if you are out there acting as though you will take whatever you can get because "beggars can't be choosers."

At the point when your own reality is negative and loaded with questions, bends and disgrace, you shout that message to the world in a great many nonverbal ways. What you accept is your "genuine article" reflects itself in your non-verbal communication, your looks and your activities, which all scheme to go against each word you say and the impression you endeavor to make.

Goodness, I get everything right. You have a set of experiences that perhaps you're not pleased with. Perhaps you've laid down with an adequate number of folks to make up two football crews — including the training crews. You might have been left standing at the altar or dumped. The fact of the matter is that everything is before and you can do nothing to change it. You can begin focusing 5% of your time on determining whether you made a mistake or received a poor deal, and 95% of your time on determining what you will do about it.

Presently, it's conceivable that you have some profoundly dug in scarring in your life like attack or misuse. Assuming these things have happened to you, your enduring is genuine and reasonable. A harmed mental self view, compromised self-esteem and negative self-truth are all not out of the ordinary. Try not to briefly downplay those encounters by letting yourself know that you must destroy up and deal with it. Those encounters can make you degrade yourself. They can prompt many years of accepting that you are harmed products who nobody would need under any circumstance other than sexual delight. While it is off-base reasoning, it is justifiable. You will most likely need to get proficient assistance to conquer that — and not on the grounds that you want it, but since you merit it. Regardless of whether you at any point structure a relationship with another person, the main relationship you will at any point have is the one with yourself. Therefore, seek assistance, if not for the sake of establishing a happy relationship, then for the sake of establishing your own happiness and peace in this life.

Getting your own reality fixed is the initial step to recognizing the Personality of You. Everything about your message, your aura, and who you are will change. If you are unsure of what constitutes your personal truth, the time has come to confront your doubts head-on:

1. Do I feel that I need to mask myself?

2. Do I live with disgrace?

3. Do I carry around guilt?

4. Do I think I'm not smart enough?

5. Is there really something wrong with me?

6. Do I need certainty?

7. Do I think my _____ (dearest companion, sister, and so forth.) is some way or another better than I'm?

8. Do I think I'm being conned?

9. Do I believe that I am a third-class citizen?

10. Do I feel shameful of adoration?

11. Do I frequently feel I have zero power over my life and conduct?

12. Am I harmed products — have I been unloaded so often that there must be some kind of problem with me?

13. Do I think I'm less interesting, smart, or sharp than other people?

14. Do I think I will never find contentment?

15. Do I share with myself that I'm not commendable?

16. Do I feel that I am disguising and only out in front of being found out?

17. Do I think that compared to my peers, I am completely clueless?

18. Do I constantly play the game out of fear of being humiliated and hurt?

I have recently taken you through an organized assessment of conceivable pessimistic substance in your own reality. The primary thing that ought to go on your plan for the day is to take out, recuperate, change, do anything that you need to do so it no longer affects you. Ideally, the majority or even most of your own truth is positive. Most of individuals have a combo bargain.

We all produce the outcomes we believe we deserve, which is why we are conducting this personal truth inventory. So on the off chance that you can dispose of, limit and deal with the negatives, you will actually want to amplify the up-sides and present the outcomes that are reliable with somebody who has positive self-esteem. To put it another way, if you don't like yourself, no one else will either. Others will love you if you love yourself. On the off chance that you accept that you merit the best relationship, you will draw in a sound, positive, satisfying relationship into your life.

Saying, "I am a quality person, so I should be treated in a quality manner" is your personal truth. So when some jerk rolls up, slaps you on the butt and says, "Hello, child, you need to take a tumble?" you can say, "Stand by a moment. Jerk, you don't talk to me that way. I merit preferred treatment over that. You address me as a woman with nobility and regard or you don't address me by any stretch of the imagination." However, on the off chance that you are staying there thinking, "Wow, I will take what I get on the grounds that no one needs me," and someone slaps you on the butt, you might think, "All things considered, essentially I'm getting grabbed and it's better compared to being distant from everyone else." Then, at that point, you're getting what you anticipate. You ought to be telling yourself, "I merit someone to invest energy with me, share encounters with me and get to know me. Not get my butt." Assuming that your own reality is negative, you will make due with being grabbed. Assuming that it is positive, you will not.

To that end I don't need the negative voices in your mind shouting stronger than the positive voices. In the event that any of the responses to the above questions is indeed, focus in and plan to accomplish some genuine work. You will need to transform each of those self-destructive responses and the perceptions that led you to them into positive, constructive thoughts if you want to truly sell yourself on yourself. Whenever you have sold yourself on you, you'll understand that you needn't bother with a man in that frame of mind to be entirety. What's more, that is getting your head in the game — coming at it with the mentality of a champ, not a washout. Since, in such a case that you're letting yourself know that you would do well to find an accomplice quick or you'll simply twist up and pass on, then you are playing with sweat-soaked palms, behaving irrationally, falling off frantic and switching folks off — and folks sense distress the manner in which a canine detects a seismic tremor; also, when they do, they take off and never think back. You've been doing fine on your own such an extremely long time, so only let it all out. It's not so alarming to go out and show the world what your identity is.

The Personality of You Passing on to Get Out

Who are you? Try not to simply overlook this inquiry. This part is basic to characterizing the Personality of You, so view it in a serious way. Give it some serious thought, and then tell me who you are. Presently record it on paper

In the event that you said an educator, an understudy, a little girl and sister, a Christian or a solitary white female, attempt once more. What are you?

I'm _____, isn't that annoying? Who are you?" is an inquiry that prompts another inquiry: " Your meaning could be a little clearer." Do you need my name? My age? My religion? My orientation? My profession? My part in my loved ones? Who I'm with my companions? The individual I am with my business partners? So many of us loathe this inquiry. We could do without expounding on ourselves, or discussing ourselves. We could do without pondering ourselves so much. And if you want to connect with someone in love, that presents a significant challenge.

Getting seen in the singles scene is tied in with reaching out to your own extraordinary person. That is your authority, and nothing else will suffice. You need to know what your identity is and disregard all the other things. At the point when I do interviews, now and again radiated through satellite to stations all around the country, I can end up conversing with many broadcasters over the course of about one day. It sometimes feels like you keep talking to the same person. Without a doubt, they have various names and come from various states, however they each have a similar bought grin, a similar perfect hair and a similar Rhonda Radio from No place USA voice. No articulation, no uniqueness, no peculiarity. The ones I recollect, the ones who truly stick out, are the ones who have a little disposition, the hot ones who are individuals first and anchors second. Also, it isn't so much that they're sullen or unpleasant, it's simply that they're not frantically attempting to eradicate their uniqueness to fit focal projecting's "columnist form."

You must be particular like this. You would rather not be any old face in the group. When the tall, thin blondes enter the room, you might think everyone is looking at them, but don't they all kind of look the same? Be somebody unmistakable. I'm not saying you ought to attempt to interest everyone. It's basically impossible that you are out there attempting to get everyone in your postal district to date you. That's simple, and the girl who does it is also simple, which is about as nice of a compliment as you can give her. We as a whole understand what we call that young lady. You are simply attempting to find that one person who has the Personality of Him that fits with the Personality of You.

Some of you are the Jennifer Aniston type: darlings with an appeal and attraction you can't resist the urge to cherish. Then, at that point, you have your Angelina Jolie hottie types. Both women have a lot of success, are very attractive, and would be attractive to a lot of men—even the same man. be that as it may, these ladies are all around as various as constantly. Because they are so different from one another, they stick out. Make an impression, that's what you have to do. Fortunately, there are a variety of ways of doing this that don't include dating Brad Pitt.

There are many ways to excel, but one surefire way to be a chump is to disappear into the background. The most exceedingly terrible thing that can happen is that you hit up a party or a get-together and the following day, a gathering of folks who were there are talking and not one of them could select you from a setup! In the event that not one of them can recall whether you were the tall young lady or the fair young lady or the young lady with the talking parrot on her shoulder just on the grounds that you neglected to have an effect of any kind, then welcome to Singleville, populace: You!

You maintain that every last one of those folks should have an exceptionally clear and particular memory of you. One might have preferred you and one more might not have really focused on you by any means, however — generally significant the two of them saw you and have no issue reviewing you and their experience of you. How would you get that this done like clockwork? Answer: You distinguish your special Person of You and structure a characterized item that you show the world. Focus on it, amplify it, embrace it and love it. That is the pony that you will ride. Certain individuals will like it and some will not, yet in the event that it is extraordinarily you and you focus on it, you will get another person to focus on it too.

This all beginnings by you tolerating that you are what your identity is. In any case, that doesn't mean you shouldn't work on yourself where and when you can. This isn't a reason to bc lethargic. Assuming you are overweight, raise it and get the additional pounds off — for your appearance, however for your wellbeing, energy, confidence and general mentality. Superficial? Perhaps, yet to win, you must work at it and take your game to a higher level. Winners do things that losers do not want to do, which is the difference between winners and losers.

Change your hair and clothes if they make you look like I Love the 80s! You don't maintain that individuals should see you and think, "Goodness, no doubt. I can recall a time when that was fashionable! Glance around, have some friendly responsiveness and get it together. Try not to let yourself know that it's alright and that it shouldn't make any difference in the event that it's not OK. It makes a difference. Change a quality if it can be changed and is worth changing! A five-year-old realizes you ought to transform it. With respect to those characteristics you can't change, similar to your level, your overall insight, your childhood and your experience, now is the right time to acknowledge it and don't think back.

Your Characterized Item

In this part, we will start further developing your game so at some point, somebody can see you strolling with your sweetheart or spouse and say, "What does she have that I haven't got — I mean, other than that extraordinary person on her arm?" At the point when that occurs, you can simply grin and give her your canine eared duplicate of this book.

I'm wagering that those young ladies you're "abhorring," the ones with the truly fair sweethearts, the ones you will resemble when we're through, either got stupid fortunate being perfectly positioned brilliantly or truly had something that you simply don't have. That something is the very thing I call a characterized item and a system for displaying it to the world. Ladies who get what they need throughout everyday life and love have sorted out their own best and most impressive mix of qualities, ways of behaving, actual properties and character attributes that separates them particularly from the wide range of various ladies on the planet. They've transformed these into their characterized item — and afterward they've worked it for everything it has.

Imagine a choir of beautiful voices that are all great but are all the same. Then a soloist moves forward and that voice transcends the rest with celestial tones. That is the very thing we have to do with you. You need to transcend the commotion. You need to turn into the figure against the backdrop of the world. You need to contrast the foundation. What's more, to do that, we should recognize the attributes that put you aside from the ladies around you and make you the soloist in the ensemble of your life.

Presently you might think, "Oh rapture, we've hit an obstacle here since I'm simply not excessively exceptional. I simply don't have those novel attributes and qualities." That is the reason I'm here — to let you know that this isn't correct. You may not see the value in your best characteristics this moment, yet we will find them before we happen to the following two parts. In all actuality, the outcome may not be what you had expected. It may not be all that you would arrange up and plug into yourself assuming you were going down a cafeteria line — "I'll take one request for that sparkly hair and an aiding of charm, please; what's more, many thanks!" You're not Ms. Potato Head, you can't stick on another nose, ears and a mouth, and the individuals who attempt wind up looking more phony than a Halloween veil — and typically a ton more frightening. In any case, I guarantee you will find that what you really do have truly deserve being adored and really focused on by someone that you love and care about. You can't keep on being the trick of the trade in your life.

Men are not dating criminal investigators. They typically do not actively seek a life partner with the same level of vigor as women. They won't come into your existence with the sole reason for surveying whether you are "the one." They won't dig and pull around searching for the attributes, characteristics and qualities that are the best fit for their extraordinary somebody. They may not understand what those attributes, characteristics and qualities are. Men will invest unending energy exploring another vehicle or a boat or which extra large television has the best picture, yet they simply don't have that relationship-marriage "chip" in their mind at similar level ladies do, which we will discuss in Part 6. That implies you must certainly stand out enough to be noticed. The answer is not to tell them what they think they want to hear. Attempting to think about what they assume they need and fill that bill isn't the response. As you are going to find out, you are not ideal for everyone. In any case, you, and not certain individuals satisfying adaptation of you, will be ideal for someone.

I can assure you that one of the main reasons why some people find the partner they're looking for and others don't is that they have accepted their Character of You and defined that character's product. This unmistakable and particular item made someone be drawn to them. Because it was real, it was powerful; it was bona fide, and it was acknowledged by them well before they chose to attempt to get it acknowledged by "him."

Everyone, including you, has a specific heavenly body of qualities and qualities that, once recognized and showed, makes a power you can't start to envision. As I stated, I don't want you to remain your life's best-kept secret. I don't need you hanging tight for "random karma." I believe that you should make your own karma.

Robin, my wife, is, in my opinion, a perfect example. I will concede that, to some extent as I would see it, she has a major upside that a many individuals don't have. She has always been a "ten" who runs smoothly. Also, I just own it was her looks that definitely stood out enough to be noticed from minute one, however when I met her and began conversing with her, I was hypnotized. She had a sort of guaranteed demeanor: " I'm who I'm, I understand what I need and in the event that you could do without it, another person will." (I actually think she was somewhat feigning and was insane in affection with me, yet she won't ever 'fess up!) She was feisty, flippant and a positive conundrum. She was not a "bad girl," and she certainly wasn't Goody Two Shoes. She was fun, unpredictable, and had a great spirit of adventure, but she was a spunky, "double dog dare ya" kind of girl.

She was unquestionably "Woohoo!" when it was time to let loose. She had a powerful and enticing connection when it was time to be quiet. Never, ever monotonous. That was her trademark item. Because it felt real at the time and hasn't changed a whit more than thirty years later, I know it was real. It distinguishes her from others. She couldn't have cared less assuming she had cosmetics on or whether her hair was flawlessly prepped or standing out in 24 headings — she was generally a similar shimmering, energetic Robin. You knew when you were with her you could never be exhausted. In no time, I was endeavoring to win her endorsement, a great spot for her to be in. I need precisely that for you.

I believe that you should be in the power position in your connections so you are the one sought after, as opposed to the follower. Also, trust me, that is the very thing you want to go for. You don't want him anyway, even if you have to chase him down like a hungry cheetah after a gazelle. Connections are intense enough when the two individuals are running toward one another; He won't let go of you if you're in a relationship where he's nervous. You want to catch his eye, show him who you can be in his life, and then let him be "Cheetah Boy." Therefore, you require an advantage. Like that, when you find the unique fellow and he finds you, he will ponder where you have been for his entire life.

You are all familiar with girls who can simply enter a room and rule it. They might not be the most beautiful people in the crowd, they might not fit the media's idea of what it means to be conventionally attractive, and they probably don't even have the most skin, but they always seem to get all the attention. Love them or disdain them. In any case, here's the key part: Certainty and self-acknowledgment are making them so brilliant, and those come just whenever you've dominated the principal rule of the game, which additionally is the main rule of deals: In the event that you're not sold on your item, you will not have the option to sell any other person on it by the same token.

You need to get right with you first. Furthermore, I don't mean simply letting yourself know a lot of rah positive reasoning. I mean truly finding your best credits, your most helpful attributes, the genuine qualities that make you unmistakable. If you're sitting there and saying things like, "Look, I know a funny girl or a good-looking girl when I see one, and I ain't it," you're not being honest. That is not a problem. That should not be the Personality of You and that is fine. I can assure you that whatever you are and whatever you have going for you are plenty good enough if you fully embrace them and show them to the world.

Most of us can distinguish ourselves. Consider me. Every day is a "bad hair day" for me! In any case, so what? How many Hollywood celebrities have you observed and wondered, "How in the world did that person ever become famous?" A valid example: DeVito, Danny The man is scarcely five feet tall, overweight and bare. In the event that you are finishing up list of references for driving men, I don't figure you will see those attributes on the short rundown. However he is a big name. Why? (1) He is talented, 2) He is likeable, and 3) He is different from everyone else in a very big way.

We wouldn't have been able to appreciate Danny's screen presence if he had sat back and said, "I have a face and body for radio." instead of participating.

"Better believe it, however he's a person," you say. " Guys have different experiences, right? Now, just take a look at someone like Kathy Bates. She may not be customarily Hollywood or extraordinarily appealing, yet she is such a charming and strong individual that you can't take your eyes off her! She is multifaceted, adorable, and funny. So don't undercut yourself since you don't satisfy the run of the mill guideline. You don't need to quantify yourself by conventional, normal principles of what makes an individual appealing and engaging.

I Have Versus What He Needs this

The normal grumbling I hear from men is that they're dating Stepford ladies. All they hear when they go out on a date is, "Oh, yes, I completely agree." At first, that seems great. Is there any good reason why you wouldn't adore somebody who prefers every one of your thoughts, giggles at every one of your jokes, centers exclusively around you and becomes involved with all that you say? However, one log won't consume.

I will tell you about something that's usually kept under wraps: men need to feel that they have worked for and acquired something, or they won't esteem it. Come and go with ease. You won't keep his attention if you give up too quickly. From the outset, being pleasing is fine and dandy, yet ultimately we need to know your real assessment, and in the event that you don't have one, you are nap city. A man might get the same thrill from picking up a coma patient as he does from you. Men only want an honest opinion. A man is content regardless of the viewpoint's divergence or even its shocking nature—as long as it is genuine, unflinching, and does not involve human sacrifice, he is content. He enjoys himself. He is curious. He is interested. He thinks he's getting to know you better.

Appears to be basic, however the truth of the matter is that an enormous level of ladies would sooner shave their heads and join the Krishnas than offer a fair viewpoint and risked switching off their date. You might be shaking your head and thinking, "Oh no, that couldn't possibly apply to me." Some of you might be doing that. All things considered, I wouldn't wager on that. Women have been conditioned to look for signs of interest from men before beginning to evaluate their own feelings because men have traditionally been the ones on the lookout. It's the old mentality: I'll expert the meeting, land the position, then, at that point, choose whether to take it" — extraordinary in business, horrible in dating. As a matter of fact, this is unequivocally the mentality that leads so many to betray dating through and through on the grounds that they can't confront the possibility of another "new employee screening" date.

Attempting to be everything to all individuals is at the base of these dull dates and shallow discussions, and it is the single greatest misstep ladies make when they are dating.

Those of you actually staying here thinking, "Indeed, consider the possibility that I simply have no extraordinary attributes." are also held accountable. Permit me to put it this way: What is awesome of what you have? I'm not saying that in the event that you had your druthers, you'd choose those characteristics from a list, yet moderately talking, given just what you need to work with, what are your long suits? Consider it in this way: On the off chance that we were lost in a woods and needed to get by, the primary thing I could ask is, What do we have? Do we have covers, a compass, flares, matches, food, a tent? On the off chance that I'm out there and I don't have a tent, I will pull branches off trees and cover myself up so I don't get frostbite. Of course, I would prefer to have a tent and a Coleman light and a decent open air fire, however I'm living in reality, so I will capitalize on what I have — two arms, two legs and an endurance nature that pushes me to build a stopgap cover.

A few ladies are great at this "utilization what the great master gave you" approach. As of late Robin and I were going to a capability at a lead representative's chateau. We were both going to give a speech in front of a distinguished group of people wearing black tie. Yet, when she opened her bag, she understood that she had brought just a single shoe. Then, at that point, in her scramble to get dressed, she broke one of the spaghetti lashes on her outfit. So we are right here: clock ticking, broken lash on outfit and one shoe. Did she overreact? No. Before I know it, she emerges from the room looking flat out amazing. I have no clue about how she got it done, yet she never thought twice. You ladies know how to make the best of what you have and you do it the entire life. Think back to every time you have done something similar, whether it was fixing that ripped hem with a glue gun or making an entire lunch out of what other people thought was an empty refrigerator. That was all groundwork for what we are referring to here, at this moment. That multitude of encounters were simply setting you up for this second in time.

With regards to characterizing yourself, there is a particular distinction between ladies who say, "This is the very thing I have" and the people who inquire, "What is it that you need?" The first are emphasizing the value they bring to the table. The last option are attempting to characterize themselves as far as their thought process individuals need — a catastrophe waiting to happen in the event that I've heard one.

I'll let you know at the present time, you won't understand what your characterized item is until you've recognized your most grounded ascribes, qualities, resources and attributes. So you want to take a stock and afterward present your discoveries to the world, rather than going around weakly attempting to be everything to all individuals. Constant individuals satisfying either brings an end to the relationship from the outset on the grounds that your potential accomplice detects your thought processes and gets exhausted, or it kills the relationship gradually, after you frustrate every one of the assumptions you've set up. At the point when Robin and I initially began dating, I told her that I play tennis. At the point when I inquired as to whether she played tennis, she said, "Gracious better believe it." So I thought, "Gracious, extraordinary, she looks perfect and a tennis player as well." So we made courses of action to play, and the primary point she made to me when she got in the vehicle was, "OK, I give. I don't have any idea how to play tennis." We both pretty much passed on snickering — and afterward I beat her in straight sets, or might have beaten her. She fessed up so rapidly that I wasn't irritated. I adored the sincerity and attitude.

There could be no surer method for fizzling than to forfeit who you are for progress, ubiquity or a relationship. Take me, for instance. I was aware as a child that I would never be like Paul Newman or Robert Redford. My nose was broken multiple times and I began going bare at 22. Model material I wasn't. However, I was large, tall, athletic and genuinely savvy. So I turned into that tall person with an extraordinary funny bone. That made me feel at ease, which made other people feel at ease around me. Perhaps you wouldn't go gaga for me from the beginning, however allow me a moment. If you are not careful, I might sneak up on you.

Since then, not much has changed. I appeared in Hollywood, where everybody is under thirty, is tan and has extraordinary hair. Actually take a look at the front of this book on the off chance that you want to revive your memory, yet that isn't what I resemble. A many individuals said, "Gracious, you're fifty, you're going bald and you have that unmistakable Texas drone; that will not work on television." However, I'll let you know right now that in this present reality where everybody is frantically attempting to seem to be Johnny Depp, appearing as though yours genuinely can mean enormous achievement. The way that I'm uncovered alone is sufficient to make me perhaps of the most conspicuous face on television. I am indeed middle-aged. Indeed, I have a one of a kind discourse design. Indeed, I'm not the handsomest fiend to at any point beauty the cinema. Why then? Assuming you're searching for beautiful sight, you have many channels to look over. Just take my for it, no mishap I'm doing a syndicated program, not a look-and-see show. You won't track down me on the WB's new hot-fellow show. I do a television show since talking is my long suit. So on the off chance that you're searching for somebody with a remark, I'm your person.

Think Unique

All in all, individuals who have never gone to considerable lengths to recognize their Personality of You and characterize their item don't respect themselves. It's as if they're still the same vulnerable eighth-grader who was teased because they had a funny shoe or bad haircut. They need to mix in rather than stick out, since, in such a case that they mix in, individuals won't see them to ridicule them or condemn them. The quintessence of the characterized item methodology opposes that kind of rationale since everything revolves around getting taken note.

It's about not accepting a Prada sack in the event that you can't stand to cover the charge card bills. It's about not consenting to go for sushi in the event that you seriously hate crude fish. About not saying you're 29 assuming that you are truly 35. You don't need to be rich. You don't need to adore sushi. You don't need to be youthful. To get along, you don't have to go along. You should simply be authentic. Trust me, there is somebody who might be listening who needs you definitively for what your identity is and what you bring to the table. You simply need to sort out what that is first.

Made in the USA
Columbia, SC
30 March 2025

55881075R20059